Skating t...

by Lee S. Justice

Strategy Focus

As you read, **evaluate** how well the author explains the history of ice skating.

HOUGHTON MIFFLIN   BOSTON

Key Vocabulary

amateur someone who does a sport for fun rather than for money

artistic creative

compete take part in a contest

elements parts; ingredients

judges people who decide who wins a contest

presentation performance

pressure strong demands

required necessary

technical having to do with skill and technique

Word Teaser

If you add one letter to this word, you can spell the word *complete*. What is the word?

For hundreds of years, people have skated on frozen lakes and rivers. Sometimes they skated to get from place to place. Sometimes they skated just for fun. After a while, skaters began to compete against each other. They raced to see who was fastest or who could skate farthest.

Ice skaters also wanted to show off their skill. They began to use the edges of their skates to cut fancy lines on the ice. The lines they made were called figures. Their sport became known as figure skating.

A First Leap

In 1909, Ulrich Salchow (SAL kow) of Sweden was skating in an important contest. Suddenly, he leaped and made a full turn in the air! Then he landed on the edge of one skate.

Today, this may not seem like such a hard thing to do. But at the time, people were amazed. No one had ever jumped in a figure skating contest. The judges were impressed, too. They gave him first prize.

Ulrich Salchow in 1925 with future Olympic skating champion Sonja Henie.

Other skaters tried Salchow's jump. They tried other jumps, too. Soon these jumps were required in skating contests. Skaters had to show the judges that they could perform these elements, or parts, of a skater's routine.

Olympic champ Sonja Henie in 1936

Taking Chances

Dick Button was twelve years old when he had his first skating lesson. Six years later, he skated in the Olympics. Button did something no Olympic skater had ever done before. He leaped off the ice and spun around two and a half times before landing!

Button's daring jumps made others want to try even harder tricks. More and more, skaters felt pressure to do new things.

Dick Button

Button later became the first skater to spin three times in the air. Today, skaters often perform this jump. Some skaters can even make four spins in the air!

Button helped make figure skating an exciting, action-packed sport. He had amazing technical skills, but he also knew how to put on a great show.

Today's skaters have great technical skills, too.

Elvis Stojko

Miki Ando

Surya Bonaly

Dance to the Music

In ice dancing, a male and a female skater glide together to music. Ice dancers have great technical skills. But presentation is very important, too. How smoothly do both skaters move across the ice? How well do their movements match the music? Ice dancing is an artistic, creative sport.

For a long time, ice dancing was a less showy event than figure skating. Nobody guessed that it would one day become the most exciting event at the Olympic Games!

At the 1984 Winter Olympics, Jayne Torvill and Christopher Dean made ice dancing into a thrilling show. They seemed to tell a story with their dance. Thousands of viewers watched in wonder. The judges gave them the highest score ever for their artistic presentation. Today ice dancing is a favorite sport in the Winter Olympics.

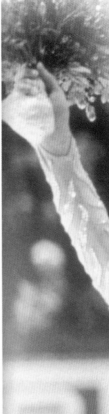

Like many other Olympic athletes, Torvill and Dean started out as amateurs. They were not paid for their skating performances. After the Olympics, they became very popular professional, or paid, performers.

What Next?

Every year, skaters try new things that seem nearly impossible. What will they do tomorrow? No one knows for sure. But we do know one thing. Skaters will continue to amaze us.

NOTE

NOTE

Putting Words to Work

1. What does it mean to perform well under **pressure**?

2. Once, only an **amateur** could skate at the Olympics. Who could not **compete**?

3. The author states that skaters "will continue to amaze us" with their **artistic** and **technical** skills. Is this a fact or an opinion? Explain your answer.

4. In a skating contest, a **required element** is _____.

5. **PARTNER ACTIVITY:** Think of a word you learned in the text. Explain its meaning to your partner and give an example.

Answer to Word Teaser

compete (add an *l*)